LITTLE MONSTER AT HOME

by Mercer Mayer

to Paul

MERRIGOLD PRESS • NEW YORK

Library of Congress Catalog Card Number: 77-90843   ISBN: 0-307-03933-1   A MCMXCI

This is my house where I live with Mom and Pop. First there is my sister and then there is me and last of all there is the baby, who can't talk yet.

In the very bottom of my house is the cellar.
It's full of machines that make hot water and heat.

And in the very top of my house is the attic.
It's full of great things that nobody uses anymore
but we keep just in case.

My house is full of rooms. The kitchen is for cooking and snacks.

I'm very neat and clean up sometimes.

In the pantry are all sorts of
cans and boxes and jars of food.
My mom makes the best apple jelly.

The living room is where we do things together. Pop reads his favorite book and Mom practices the violin. I bet I have the only mom in town who practices the violin.

Sometimes my sister and I play checkers. She usually wins. My pet Kerploppus sleeps on the couch, even though he is not supposed to.

When I have friends over, we go to the playroom. That way Mom isn't always telling us to be quiet. We watch TV and play games. The playroom is mainly for noise, and if you don't like noise, you'd better stay with Mom and Pop. They don't like noise either.

We have a workshop in the garage. Pop is making a little Croonie house. I am painting a stool for Mom.

The laundry room is where my clothes
go when they get dirty.

And the bathroom is where
I go when I get dirty.

This is my room. It's full of all my very own stuff. No one is allowed in here except Mom and Pop and my pet Kerploppus, and my best friend. Not even my sister, but sometimes I lend her my baseball bat.

In the spring at my house, we take down the storm windows and put up screens to keep out the bugs. We plant our vegetable garden and beat the rugs. Everyone helps except my Kerploppus. He just gets in the way.

We throw away old stuff we don't want anymore. I always find lots of things I want to save, but Mom won't let me.

GARBAGE MONSTER PLEASE PICK UP

In the summer, we work in the yard. Pop prunes the apple tree, Mom cuts the grass, my sister trims the hedge, and I weed the garden.

In the fall, we pick apples for Mom's apple jelly. We get a pumpkin from the garden for a jack-o'-lantern. Pop works on the house and Mom rakes the leaves. I jump into the piles.

In the winter, it's too cold to stay outside for long, but at Christmastime Grandma and Grandpa come and we all go out and cut down our Christmas tree.

I like my house best in the wintertime because
when we get inside it's so very snuggly and warm.